Happy

BY SAVINA COLLINS

ILLUSTRATED BY
ANITA DUFALLA

Rourke
Educational Media
rourkeeducationalmedia.com

Before & After Reading Activities

Teaching Focus:

Concepts of Print: Ending Punctuation- Have students locate the ending punctuation for sentences in the book. Count how many times a period, question mark, or exclamation point is used. Which one is used the most? What is the purpose for each ending punctuation mark? Practice reading these sentences with appropriate expression.

Before Reading:

Building Academic Vocabulary and Background Knowledge

Before reading a book, it is important to set the stage for your child or student by using pre-reading strategies. This will help them develop their vocabulary, increase their reading comprehension, and make connections across the curriculum.

1. Read the title and look at the cover. *Let's make predictions about what this book will be about.*
2. Take a picture walk by talking about the pictures/photographs in the book. Implant the vocabulary as you take the picture walk. Be sure to talk about the text features such as headings, the Table of Contents, glossary, bolded words, captions, charts/diagrams, or index.
3. Have students read the first page of text with you then have students read the remaining text.
4. Strategy Talk – use to assist students while reading.
    - Get your mouth ready
    - Look at the picture
    - Think…does it make sense
    - Think…does it look right
    - Think…does it sound right
    - Chunk it – by looking for a part you know
5. Read it again.

Content Area Vocabulary
Use glossary words in a sentence.

ballet
dream
giggle
goal

After Reading:

Comprehension and Extension Activity

After reading the book, work on the following questions with your child or students in order to check their level of reading comprehension and content mastery.

1. *What does Mia think about when she can't go to sleep? (Summarize)*
2. *What makes Mia giggle? (Asking Questions)*
3. *What are a few things that make you happy? (Text to self connection)*
4. *What ice cream flavor makes Mia happy? (Asking Questions)*

Extension Activity

Find photographs of yourself when you were happy. On the back of each photo write what made you happy. Keep the photos in a box or book and pull them out whenever you are feeling sad.

Table of Contents

Bedtime...................................... 4

Happy... 8

Picture Glossary....................23

About the Author..............24

Bedtime

It's bedtime.

4

Mia can't go to sleep.

Mia is afraid she will have a bad **dream**.

6

"Think of everything that makes you happy," Mom says.

7

Happy

Mia closes her eyes tightly.

She thinks and thinks.

She thinks about riding her
bike.

Riding faster than her brother makes her happy!

Mia thinks about dance class.

She likes **ballet** best.

Strawberry ice cream makes Mia happy.

The sweet taste makes her smile.

Mia thinks about her friends.

Their jokes make her **giggle.**

Playing soccer makes Mia happy.

She thinks about scoring a **goal**.

Helping people makes Mia happy.

She thinks about their hugs.

Sweet dreams make Mia happy. Good night!

Picture Glossary

 **ballet** (BAL-ay): A style of dance that uses precise, graceful movements.

 **dream** (dreem): Thoughts that happen in a person's mind during sleep.

 **giggle** (gig-uhl): To laugh lightly in a silly way.

 **goal** (gohl): Scoring points for getting a ball in the goal net.

About the Author

Savina Collins lives in Florida with her husband and 5 adventurous kids. She loves watching her kids surf at the beach. When she is not at the beach, Savina enjoys reading and taking long walks.

Meet The Author!
www.meetREMauthors.com

Library of Congress PCN Data

Happy/ Savina Collins
(I Have Feelings!)
ISBN 978-1-68342-143-6 (hard cover)
ISBN 978-1-68342-185-6 (soft cover)
ISBN 978-1-68342-216-7 (e-Book)
Library of Congress Control Number: 2016956533

Rourke Educational Media
Printed in the United States of America, North Mankato, Minnesota

Edited by: Keli Sipperley
Cover design and interior design by: Rhea Magaro-Wallace

Also Available as: